A Cornish Saga

H J BURGESS

Published by H J BURGESS, 2023.

This is a work of fiction. Similarities to real people, places, or events are entirely coincidental.

A CORNISH SAGA

First edition. May 27, 2023.

Copyright © 2023 H J BURGESS.

ISBN: 979-8223279839

Written by H J BURGESS.

A CORNISH SAGA
By Henry James Burgess
Preface

Over the centuries, privateers, and piracy at sea with well-documented accounts of their swashbuckling have provided countless generations' endless enjoyment.

Legendary figures such as Blackbeard have evoked images of blood-curdling exploits. Not condemned for their brutality but exalted to heroic prominence.

This is the previously untold story of a sequence of events that brought disaster to many residents of the villages and hamlets inland from the Cornish town of St. Keverne. It may upset some readers with some disturbing revelations but can inspire those who seek something for nothing to take an honest path.

The Manacles reef juts out for half a mile from the coastline and is only seen at low tide. So as the story begins you will discover how greed and poverty go hand in hand to wreck passing ships upon the rocks.

Who would have imagined it would lead to one of the most horrifying episodes ever recorded?

Part 1

Jane Martin, an insignificant woman stands motionless on the bluff of the cliff with a dirty sheepskin pulled over her head and shoulders. Her body was wrapped likewise in dirty shrouds, her lower legs and feet covered with oilskin and bound tightly with strapping. A dark ominous sky surrounds this forbidding place, and the vicious wind pounds her frail body, but no amount of punishment will move her. This aged mortal is here for a purpose and soon her fortitude will be rewarded.

Out there in the distance a schooner with three masts and sails set lengthways fore-and-aft fights the roaring waves as the currents push it closer to the shore. The combination of high spring tides and a south-westerly would bring a bounty onto the outcrop of rocks set just beneath the surface and stretching out from the coastline for at least half a mile. Known as the 'Manacles' it had proved an uncompromising adversary. Many vessels had taken the challenge and lost with disastrous outcomes.

Time is on Jane's side and as the stricken craft starts to flounder, she takes the short walk along the undulating path to alert the men who sit in relative comfort. Taking a final swig of their ale they leave the Miners Arms and assemble outside the nearby church. The dark clouds have now gone as the tide turns and the sky is now lit by a full moon. The men are joined by several women summoned from the hovels that most are born into. This is a mission that needs all hands to work together in a well-rehearsed scheme. One by one they enter the graveyard and disappear behind a high monument. On the rocky shoreline below, each member of the group which now numbered 30 or more emerges as if by magic. A secret route had taken them down unseen by anyone that may witness the deeds yet to come.

The schooner, now well seated on the rocky outcrop rolls back and forth with the now receding sea that had relentlessly battered the solid oak sides of the hull until it could take no more. Finally, the sound of rigging releasing its tension reverberates, and the vessel surrenders. The foaming sea beckons the crew and en masse they jump overboard. Swimming against the force of the outgoing current is too much for some and as lungs fill with icy water they sink beneath the waves. The creaking mass is now completely broken up; the stern the only part left that is recognisable and high on top is a figure of a man. The captain, in true tradition, is going down with his ship. An enormous wave abruptly dislodges him and sends him crashing down to meet his maker.

As for those who managed to beat the elements they scramble onto the shore. Crawling towards the waiting throng, their arms held out and looking upward into the eyes of these angels of mercy. A smile greets each one, but an iron bar lifted high strikes down upon their head with such force it splits open their brains; blood spills out, clouding the rock pool and spoiling the kelp clinging to the edges.

Over the next two hours the tide has completely turned, and the remains of the ship were clearly visible; the cargo scattered over a vast area on a now calm sea. At this point, the assembled crowd set about the retrieval of everything they can. Wading out into shallow water the men gather up the goods and stack them on the beach. The women move them onward to a safe place in the many caves that exist on this coastline. By morning, as the sun peers over the horizon, a mist has engulfed the water's edge, and again as if by magic the scavengers have gone. An early morning walker remarks to his companion that the Manacles never looked better, and a sense of serenity prevails.

Meanwhile, the men arrive back whence they came, and the landlord known only as Morgan reopened the pub. A hearty breakfast of oatmeal porridge followed by a cut of meat with boiled potato. All this washed down with a good measure of ale and a glass of rum. Time passes quickly and the men are edging to go home, it had been a long night and their beds were calling.

Suddenly, the front door bursts open, and a cloud of mist fills the entrance. A tall and very bedraggled man steps in. His mighty frame falters and he falls to the floor dropping the small casket he was carrying at his feet.

'It's the Captain' a man cries from the back of the room.

Morgan moves to help but is pulled back by several of the men.

'We can't let him see us, he's a witness to last night' another voice says but Morgan insists on dealing with this inert body lying before him.

It takes five of them to lift him onto the seat in the corner where he slowly wakes up. A glass of locally produced rum is proffered and is duly swallowed in one gulp. This liquor was renowned to send men crazy, but here this stout mariner drank with gusto. Topping up the glass Morgan asks what happened and why he was in such a state. The captain looks around the room; all eyes are scowling at him. He drinks his rum and puts the glass on the table. Everyone is holding their breath at what he may say. Would he recognize anyone? Taking a long time to speak he finally announces he cannot remember a thing. Muffled sighs ring through the room and the men slowly sit back down.

The landlord continues to enquire how he came to be here in the pub. Scratching his head he still could not say. He did remember his ship The Peregrine was in trouble in a storm but nothing after that until he found himself climbing up the cliff wall and seeing a light made for the pub. A meal was given to him, and the attic room was prepared upstairs.

After he had retired to the room the locals spent some time debating and arguing.

'I don't trust him' said one, another cautioned that

'If he regained his mind, he could spell disaster to everyone who was at the wreck. He could bring the officers of the law down on us in a wink'

Reluctantly they all agreed the risk was not worth it and a plan was hatched to dispatch him as soon as possible.

'He will be asleep for a long time yet' Morgan said

'The amount of rum he took was enough to knock out a horse'

The men left and Morgan went into the back kitchen. Stoking the open fire, he placed another log onto the embers and then settled into a large armchair where he quickly dozed off.

Within the hour a small group of men returned and secreted beneath their flowing coats were all manner of weapons. Creeping quietly up the stairs they entered the bedroom and set upon the captain. He awoke to find them stabbing him in the chest; his sturdy leather jacket and thick woollens prevented the blade penetrating fully into his flesh. He lashes out with his fists and the men return blow for blow until the man standing at the head of the bed brings it to an end as he bashes the captain's skull repeatedly with a cudgel until this powerful and courageous man fell back. He never stood a chance and was soon beyond this life. The body was carried away into the mist that still hung over this place. Across the graveyard, they stumbled with this great weight and arrived behind the church. There was a large stone tomb with the top pushed aside revealing a deep cavernous pit. A final lift of this poor soul sees him unceremoniously thrown down the hole.

The night and now the day had seen one of the dastardly deeds of many a year but not one man seemed remorseful. As they left several large black birds settled on the tombstone and sounded off a loud screeching. The men resumed their normal routines as if nothing had taken place.

Some weeks later, in the town of St. Keverne, a small town just inland from the notorious Manacles, a coach arrives pulled by four magnificent dapple-grey horses; not the usual worn-out nags that worked the land and pulled the carts about their daily grind. The ornate brasses that adorned these beasts were only surpassed by the presentation of the coach itself. Although dusty from its journey here it did not detract from the time and effort that had obviously been spent by the liveryman who kept this carriage in fine order. The coachman pulled at the reigns and brought the carriage to a halt outside the town hall.

A motley crowd immediately gathered and awaited this dignitary to alight. The footman dressed as the coachman in a blue uniform with piped edging in red silk jumps down from the rear and opens the door. A sense of expectation filled the air, and they were not disappointed when finally, a gloved hand emerged followed by a gentleman of distinction. Stepping out onto the gravel road, his clean leather shoes dulled as dust enveloped them. His elaborate clothes of fine design and workmanship signified a man who did not leave the privileges of city grandeur unless it was important. So why was he here?

Moving forward he speaks to a woman supporting her arched body with a crutch. This old hag was like many who had spent a lifetime in the fields or down the tin mines having worked themselves to death. He spoke in soft tones and enquired

'Where may I find a clean hostelry and good food?'

The woman smiled broadly as both questions were alien to her. She now slept beneath the stars and had not seen a square meal in years. The nearest she had come was by drinking the dregs of wine bottles thrown out into the yard at the rear of the pub, but these upset her stomach.

'I know where to go' calls a boy dressed in tatters.

'Then, lead on young man'

The lad jumps upon the carriage and directs them towards the coast. Along the track, they go and upon reaching the little hamlet at the edge of town they come upon the Miners Arms. The footman climbs down again and walks the few yards on tiptoe, the mud being quite soft and sticky. With a hesitant stance, he helps the gent out of the carriage and supports his arm until by the pub doorway.

Upon entering he is impressed with the welcoming ambience and sends his footman who had followed behind back to the coach to bring his belongings. A small group of urchins dressed in ill-fitting rags gather around the footman and offer to help carry the cases; reluctantly after extensive begging, he agrees and hands them a case each. As they make their way, one by one the urchins fade into thin air, along with the cases they carried. By the time the footman arrived at the pub, he was alone.

The gent now greeted by Morgan looks for somewhere to seat himself. A young pot man is sent over to dust a seat in the bay window and wipe the spilled ale off the table.

'Here my lord' as his outstretched arm points the way.

'Thank you, and what vittles' can a well-travelled visitor expect?'

'I'll see to that' said Morgan, who just returned from briefly disappearing into the back room and now wore a clean shirt and had brushed his hair.

An array of meats and a bottle of fine wine are placed before the gent. Unbeknown to him was the fact that all the fare set on the table was on board another unfortunate ship only two days previous. Having eaten his fill, he settled back with a pipe of tobacco, also provided by Morgan, and dwelled on this remarkable scene.

'How is it that such produce finds its way to these here parts?' he asked wryly.

'The seas hereabouts are kind to us and often surrender such wealth' Morgan replied.

The questioning continued for a while and the gent gradually became aware that his search was nearing its end. Morgan was now suspicious about the gent and asked about his business in St. Keverne.

'My name is Jacob Weisman, and I am here to discover what happened to a ship called The Peregrine'

Standing erect Morgan moved away from the table and rethought what he had just told him.

'What I meant to say is that no cattle have fallen over the cliff lately'

This did not account for the wine or the tobacco, so again the gent looked at him with distrust and in doing so Morgan lost his nerve, made an excuse, and fled to the kitchen.

During this exchange, the locals had stood outside, faces pressed against the windows. Now the townsfolk knew why such a dignitary had come to this backwater, they dissolved into the narrow streets and busied themselves with efforts to check that no remnants of the lost ship were evident.

The footman approaches the gent and gives him the news of his stolen belongings.

'Yes, this is the place alright,' said Jacob

Then instructs the footman that his coachman be warned without delay not to leave the coach or the horses alone and to sleep with them for fear of them going the same way. Thought to himself, this is not the quiet little Hamlet he'd imagined, and the challenge now would be to discover the truth. Where had the crew disappeared to and what of the captain? Surely someone would know the answers.

Moving across the room he sat with a small group of locals and entered conversation. It immediately became apparent that they were not going to talk with him and even the offer of free ale did not sway them. So, in the blink of an eye, they were gone, leaving him alone to ponder his crusade.

After a while, a couple of men crossed the room and made his acquaintance.

'I'm George and my friend is known as Blackie, since he works in the foundry up yonder, a filthy place to be sure' He offered them a drink which they accepted, and Morgan was summoned to make up the order. George asks Jacob why he had travelled to the town and was asking after The Peregrine, as no one had come near nor bye before.

Jacob now filled with wine took his time to answer and finally explained the crew had never been heard of and the captain never filed a report.

'Maybe it was lost in one of the storms that beset this coast,' said Blackie.

George agreed and added

'Strong currents can take a whole ship and its crew leaving so sign it ever existed'

'So, you think it was taken by the sea?' said Jacob quizzically

'Well, it has been known before' said George as he turned his head away.

Jacob, even in his intoxicated state realized that these men were not being open about what they knew, so to raise their interest spoke in a hushed voice

'It's such a shame that the treasure will never be found then'

Clearly, this had an effect as the men looked at each other and then after a few whispers announced that they could find the information for him. They asked for as much detail as to when and where the ship set sail, its destination, and its cargo would also be important especially any valuables on board.

'Well, there was truly little cargo on board, mainly furniture and domestic goods bound for Ireland'

Looking confused and annoyed Blackie started to leave

'Well, I'm not wasting my time on a pile of cooking pots and table to put them on,

'Yes, that's not worth it' said George but remained seated as he still had a full jug of ale to finish.

Jacob sensed their frustration and added that the main object of interest was a consignment for the Crown.

'That can only mean one thing - Gold' stuttered Blackie now standing to the side of Jacob.

George tells him not to speak so loudly and asks Jacob if it is true. He nodded and the pair quietly rejoiced and ordered up another drink.

After the merriment had died down Jacob suggests that they meet here again tomorrow as he was not feeling very well

'Maybe it's the ale or the day has been longer than I'm used to'

Begging his apologies, he leaves them and asks Morgan to give them another bottle he staggers up the narrow stairs to his room. Not having the strength to undress he dropped onto the straw-filled bed and fell into a deep sleep.

The next day, long before Jacob arose, the same men returned with others and were knocking at the door of the hostelry. Morgan still in his long johns opened the door and was brushed aside as the men forced their way in. Hustling Morgan through into the back kitchen they demanded food and drink. Feeling threatened he brought several bowls from the washing area and filled them with meat stew; it was still warm from sitting by the fire through the night.

As they dipped their bread Morgan sheepishly asked what was going on.

'Glad you asked that' said the one with the squint eyes.

'Information, my friend, that's what we want,' said George.

'But I know of nothing that would be of interest to you'

'Well, that's as maybe, but you're going to tell us anyway' said Blackie sitting down by the fire.

'Tell you what?'

'Think back to last winter and the ship that came to grief'

'Well, I do remember but how can I help?'

'The captain stayed here, didn't he?'

'Yes, but what has that to do with me?'

'He carried a small casket when he entered this place but when he departed there was no sign of it'

'I don't know'

A bearded man moved towards Morgan and with his large and distorted hand gripped him around the neck. The man took pleasure as he squeezed Morgan and as he choked, cried out

'I was in my slumbers when he left, so how would I know?'

The squinty man did not believe him and ordered his henchmen to extract the truth.

An hour later they had gained no further knowledge of the casket, so giving Morgan a final kicking they left. Collecting himself up from the floor Morgan washed the blood from his face and collapsed into the armchair where he lay half conscience. The footman eventually found him and gave support until Morgan could stand. Jacob was soon to learn the events of the morning and decided that it was not safe to be in these parts any longer. Hurriedly he prepared for the journey and was gone by noon.

Later, the locals were banging at the door for their usual food and drink, so reluctantly Morgan let them in. The session was difficult as pain racked his body and spat up much blood in the kitchen sink. By three thirty he was able to close, locking the doors firmly. Although still in great discomfort Morgan still had the ability to think. He did so for some time and concluded that if the roughnecks who attacked him did not have the casket, then it must be in the room that the captain occupied that fateful night.

Stumbling up the staircase he entered the room. This attic room was without a window and Morgan lit a lantern to aid his search. Shadows danced about the room and an evil presence-soaked coldness into his broken body. This did not dissuade him, and he pulled the bed from the wall. Feeling in the gap he pricked his finger on a splinter of wood and behold there was damage to the wall panelling. Blood poured from his finger as he pulled at the wall.

Finally, a hole was exposed and with his lamp now flickering through lack of oil he grasped the casket within and laid it on the bed. Lifting the lid, he just caught a glimpse of the contents before the lamp went out. The coins shone brightly even in such poor light.

'This is what it is all about' Morgan said

and now thought the beating was worth it if now he could benefit from such wealth. His dreams could now be fulfilled and a life such as his recent eminent visitor Jacob savoured could be his. Fearful that the attackers may return he replaced the casket and covered the hole. The men did not return, and this pleased Morgan, but his health suffered from the beating, and in two days he was dead. The treasure had claimed its second victim.

It was soon discovered that Morgan had been attacked by villains looking for the captain's treasure. The men had bragged about the assault when they arrived at another drinking house later that same day. This was their downfall and were soon apprehended by the military.

At their trial, they explained the existence of the treasure had led them to seek answers from Morgan. The judge, when summing up commented on the injuries sustained and that Morgan had died in agony. His assailants were all hung for his murder.

The location of the treasure was to remain a mystery and rumours that the captain had placed a curse on anyone who sought his treasure began to evolve.

A new landlord had been appointed and promoted the history which attracted many visitors to the pub. This came to the notice of Logan Rowe, the owner, and landlord of the Blue Anchor Inn at Helston. He was expanding the reach of his brewery and could see the potential of the history that now made St Keverne so popular. His 'Spingo Ale' was already a best seller and it travelled well. So, as the sun just popped up over the rooftops, he loaded up a barrel of this fine ale and along with his brewer Trevik made the journey to the Miners Arms.

It was early evening before they arrived and were met with a welcome meal. After many conversations, the barrel was brought into the pub and set to rest for tomorrow. The evening went well for Logan, and it was agreed that if the locals enjoyed the new ale, it would become a regular offering. They settled down for a good session drink and by the time closing came both Logan and Trevik were exhausted. Fortunately, visitors were few that week so vacant beds being offered came with gratitude.

The locals soon heard of the new ale and the place was full by a quarter past opening. Logan sitting in the bay window seat looked around and concluded a successful event. The barrel which contained at least 250 pints would not last for more than a day or so at this rate. So, it was agreed to send word to the brewery that more would be needed. Trevik was dispatched and Logan settled down to get to know the regular drinkers.

Following the ale's success, it was agreed to improve the Masons Arms old brewery equipment which was converted to Logans specification to avoid transporting ale across the land. Using a different water source did change the finished ale but a price reduction eased the locals to accept it.

Following the trial of the group responsible for Morgans's death representation to have a local state-funded police force was sent to parliament. It would be 5 years before they acted, and a new law brought forward by Sir Robert Peel empowered local people to set up law and order arrangements in their area.

This had several outcomes, in particular, the wrecking of ships on the Manacles. The newly appointed constables were originally involved in the acts so feared for their new paid positions if they spoke of the past.

It did place them in an awkward position though and a lenient approach was made to enforce the law. Drinking after hours was the first noticeable law to be relaxed.

It would be many years before the past deeds were consigned to history.

Part 2

The year is now 1900. 70 years had passed since those dreadful events and the passage of time has done little to improve the lives of the people who try to make a living in this wasteland. The fabric of the town had improved though with a new library, a community hall, and a boarding school for those who could afford the fees. The working conditions locally had not changed, in fact, had become worse after the tin mines closed.

Old ways found willing hands to commit crimes against humanity. Wrecking on the coast now took on a new dimension with devious means and deception to bring passing ships onto the Manacles. Coastal lights used to assist navigation were moved or falsely created to mislead and confuse. The law prohibited this but as in days gone by proving whether an accident or a deliberate act brought about a disaster was difficult. The harvest that the seas offered was considered a viable option to starving locals, who without work and the means to support their families considered they didn't have a choice.

The mines used to provide much work for the men folk, but roof collapses and gas poisonings were frequent, leaving many women without a breadwinner. This prompted them to participate actively in the recovery of the stricken ship's bounty.

Unlike in previous times, the survivors of these events were taken to safe lodgings before any cargo was removed so persuading the crew that all was lost to the waves was easy. The fact that they were alive sent them homeward bound in good spirits.

Investigators had occasionally called the area but were reassured that nature had prevailed with no evidence to denote wrongdoing. Any poor soul that lost his life during such circumstance would be given due reverence and be buried in the local churchyard. The cruel sea drowned many, but it only took a simple infection of the lung to bring an end to the newest landlord Arthur Penhaligon. It had been several years since a major brewery company bought the Masons Arms from the Rowe family.

The funeral took place nearby the home he had known since birth. He would be remembered for his generosity and the way he supported the poor that fell on challenging times, providing them with shelter and a meal. Whole families would beg succour at his door and be sustained with lamb stew and rye bread.

Now though, this man lay at rest, encased in a satin-lined oak coffin; still stained with the mark of tar, a stark reminder that a coffin could be made from any timber, even from a shipwreck.

'For heaven's sake' a voice cries out

'Be careful, lest ye want to be first in'

Sam, the grave digger issued a warning to keep away from the edge of the freshly dug hole. Overnight rain had created a quagmire and left pools of muddy water everywhere. Looking into the open void that was to be Arthur's final resting place the priest whispered to himself.

'If the poor soul was not dead already, then he would surely drown down there'

About a foot of water lay at the bottom of the grave and the sound of splashing could be heard as the sides crumbled away. The priest's short sermon was followed by an invitation for anyone to say a few words but was met with silence. As he looked around the gathering, eyes met, and heads dropped; nobody wanted to prolong the moment.

The winter weather was turning nasty and the quicker they could get away the better. Respect for the dead is one thing but getting soaked to the skin was another. Lowering the coffin down it floated for a moment and then dipped at one end as air rushed out. When it settled, Sam stepped forward and presented the priest with a casket of dry soil, held back from his dig.

After tossing a handful over the coffin the priest gathered up his gown, now sodden from the bottom up to the knees, and urged others to partake in this ritual. The rain now came vigorously and after following his example the crowd formed a scrum to leave this place of the dead. The priest is knocked down by them as they retreat and almost fall into the hole to join the departed corpse.

Many of the men make their way back to the pub to partake of the promised free drink. A new landlord had already taken over the reins and the ale flowed generously. A man of considerable experience John Master's had been sent in by the brewery to cover while poor Arthur was ill.

As the evening approached many of the mourners had taken their fill of ale and left. Only a few remained and noting that one old man seated in the bay window had not been at the funeral John poured himself a well-earned drink and asked if he may sit with him. Tom as he was known agreed and John settled down in a chair.

Introductions over, John starts the conversation and suggests the day went well. Tom sips his beer and says nothing in reply. John senses that something is wrong and asks

'Did you not get on with Arthur, then?'

Tom responded forcefully and without hesitation

'I did, he was a good friend, but I'll not be standing out in that wind catching the same chill that took him before his time'

John apologised for his assumption and offers Tom a tot of rum. He accepts and after fetching it from the bar Tom continues to explain other reasons for his reluctance to attend funerals.

'The goings on in that graveyard are enough to frighten a man to death'

John sat thinking of what to say next in case he upset him again. Tom, drinking the rum with one swig offers a piece of advice

'Best you think again about staying here, the omens are not good for you'

Before John could muster a response, the old harbinger was gone.

In the months that followed John enquired about the pub and its history. Much was known about the dark days when tales of ritual beatings, sacrifice, and cannibalism were supposed to have occurred. There were accusations about the local church and its involvement with a secret society but nobody had any proof so whatever did happen remains a mystery. However, the pub didn't seem to have a direct link to such goings on but if the same perpetrators went to the church just a stone's throw away it seemed logical, they spent time in the pub as well. He was not a well-educated man, but John had common sense, and this led him away from believing the unfounded gossip.

As it was Sunday, he looked forward to seeing Tom again since he was the only one who could cast light on these rumours. Mrs. Emmin, a well-preserved widow in her later years had been engaged as a cook to prepare the roast of the day. John always found it far too difficult to get everything ready to serve simultaneously, especially keeping things right during a lunch session. Complaints about the food had affected his takings so here she was to put things right and this she did with consummate ease.

Seeing John constantly looking out the window she asked

'Is there something wrong?'

Taking another glance out he turned to her

'No' he said hesitantly

'Well, for someone without trouble, you certainly give the impression of someone who is expecting it'

'No, it's just that I thought Tom may have been here for his lunch by now'

Sighing loudly, she cynically said

'Ah, is that all'

John made his way toward the bar and poured several drinks for those waiting. Having done so, he returned to the window and kept a watchful eye on the path from Tom's home.

'He'll know when the food is ready' Mrs. Emmin called out from the kitchen.

'Why, is he psychic?' John said sarcastically

'No, he's not psychic; it's just that if the wind is blowing from the east, he can smell my cooking wafting in the air'

John peered around the kitchen door and grinned at her.

Moments later, there on the path was the man himself. Now much slower than he used to be old age and the winter cold taking its toll on his frail body. Once inside he stood at the polished oak bar to order his usual meal and a jug of ale. John shouted the order through to Mrs. Emmin and then took the money from Tom's crumpled hand; pained by arthritis. As John gave him his change Tom said in an accusing voice

'You've not taken enough money'

'The ale is on the house' said John warmly

Tom had declined free ale before knowing that John would press him for information about the past but now as money was tight, he accepted. Shrugging his shoulders, he ambled over to his usual seat and set the jug on the table.

During the next hour, John found time to sit with Tom and asked him directly

'Why did you warn me to not stay in the pub when I first met you?'

Tom looked up from the now empty plate still set before him.

'So, you did hear me then' he said wryly

'Well, yes I did'

'Does it worry you? asked Tom inquisitively

'No, but it interests me that you gave no reason at the time and haven't mentioned it since'

Tom pulled John by the sleeve towards him and in lowered voice said

'No, well some things are best left alone save you stir up the past'

John was needed back at the bar, so did not reply, but later as Tom was leaving John managed to catch him for a moment.

'Yes, but flesh-eating orgies that take some believing'

'Well, let me tell thee that many generations may have distorted the truth, but the written accounts from the time are a different matter' explained Tom

'So, there's a record of these crimes?'

'Yes, at the library in the town' Tom uttered as he opened the door and stumbled away along the path.

Returning to his duties John put to one side all thoughts of what he had been told as there would be plenty of time to seek the truth.

A few days later, John found time to go into the town centre and with help from the locals found the library. Frustrated by the locked entrance doors he crossed the road and entered the tea rooms. A friendly female greets him and directs him to a seat by the fire and takes his order

'A scone and a pot of tea, please'

'Yes, sir, and will that be all?'

'Yes, thank you' and thinking quickly

'There is something though, could you tell me if the library will be open today?'

Placing her notebook into the pocket of her apron as she turns

'It opens promptly at 10 this morning'

Then having returned to the counter, pours hot water into the pot along with another spoonful of loose tea and lifting the lid of the glass display dome lifts a scone from beneath.

Now served and with only 20 minutes to wait John tucks into his tea and scone. He contemplates his mission and wonders whether the librarian will think him silly with such naive, wild ideas, particularly at his age of 28 years. From the window, half covered by curtaining he could see the library doors swing open wide, a fresh-faced woman glanced up and down the street and retreated inside. John knew he was going to make his inquiries now, such a vision of loveliness he had not seen before and wanted to meet her.

Brushing the crumbs from his coat he thanked the waitress and strode towards the ornate stone arch that adorned the library entrance. Gargoyles, high up looked down on him and followed his every step. Once inside he removed his cap, rolled it, and put it in his pocket. Joining the short queue and running his fingers through the unkempt hair he slowly edged forward. With only one person in front of him, his eyes followed the young library assistant as she opened the books before stamping them with a date.

She was incredibly beautiful and when finally, at the front found himself lost for words. He struggled to make any sense and realizing he was flustered she touched the back of his hand with her long immaculate fingers

'Take a deep breath and relax'

He melted at hearing her sweet voice talking to him as well. Eventually his reason for being there was made clear, and she asked him whether he wanted to join or just read the books here in the library.

'Join' he said urgently and continued

'If you please'

When this formality was complete and after all the others waiting after him in the queue had been dealt with, she accompanied him to seek out the books that may contain the information he desired. Along the narrow aisles, they went until the reference section, where she pulled several volumes off the shelves. Placing them on a nearby table

'There, that should keep you going for a while and if what you seek is not there, then let me know'

His hands were shaking as he opened the first book that looked likely to contain something of interest. The title 'The Fisherman of Penzance' is a work of interest to anyone learning how to fish the south coast but not how the people went about their daily lives, but nothing about crimes against humanity. So, having taken off his coat began to read the other books, but this led nowhere.

Eventually, he went back to speak to the librarian who he now knew as Miss Pascoe. Having calmed since meeting her he was able to explain in more detail that which he sought. Being knowledgeable in local history she found the items he wanted and suggested that as a member he could take them home to read. Knowing this would end his time in her presence he reluctantly withdrew the 3 books and as he was leaving, she asked

'Did you enjoy the scones?' and added

'I like them as well'

Looking down his front he could see no evidence of the tearoom delights he had sampled earlier. Raising a small handkerchief, she wiped the crumbs and jam from the edge of his mouth. They smiled at each other and in his embarrassment tripped over the entrance step as he made his retreat. Turning at the curb he looked back and gained another smile and a little wave.

Encouraged by the success of his enterprise he returned to the pub and toasted his good fortune with a glass of the finest whisky. John had been uncertain of himself and his future here in the remoteness of the West Country but now he pictured his destiny and would stay. He believed that Miss Pascoe could be the one he could settle down with and start a family.

Seated in his armchair he began reading the books and it was not long before he touched upon the rumours that abound in this town and the pub. He continued to read and soon forgot the time. A loud banging on the front door upset the intensity of his task and the pub evening session would prevent him from finding the answers until later. When the pub finally closed, he left the mess in the bar and returned to his exploration of the past. It referred to an assortment of misdeeds and even mentioned cult followers offering up sacrifice but nothing about any treasure or curse. Being Thursday, he would not see Tom for days until he came for his Sunday roast, so his doubts would have to wait for an answer.

John slept uneasily that night and awoke early only to find the pub in a real state with dirty glasses and uneaten food still on plates scattered around the bar and kitchen. The smell was indescribable and gave rise to a feeling of imminent vomiting and even the chilly air that blew in through the now-open window could disguise it. So, he decided to have a proper spring clean even if it was late September.

After washing the pots and wiping down the tables he set about the bar. Since arriving he had never really given it the benefit of a sort out and could see dust piled up in all the unused corners. Pulling out the old boxes from under the bar counter large insects scurried into the cracks in the timber which made him jump. Half-used candles, a broken jug and something he could not distinguish which had previously been covered in a thick mould but was now dried to leave a crust were pulled out and then he came upon a small leather pouch. Dry and brittle it had been there for many years and was difficult to unfasten. Tipping the contents out he stood back in amazement. There, as distinct as the day it was made was a coin, a gold coin. Taking a closer look, he finds it has the date of 1827 and the image of a man's head. Not someone he recognised and written in a foreign tongue. John puzzled over its origin, and this would be another mystery to solve.

Tom arrived as usual on Sunday following the aroma that flowed from Mrs. Emmin's cooking. As he placed his order John emptied the pouch in front of him. Tom never flinched and just looked at John.

'Well, what do you think?' asked John expectantly

Picking it up and rolling it around from side to side for a moment Tom said

'Portuguese, I think'

'I found it under the bar last night and was hoping you might know how it came to be there'

'How would I know?' Tom was in no mood for guessing games.

John, now disappointed passed the order through to the kitchen and returned to find Tom had picked up the coin again. Without saying anything John poured a jug of ale and presented it to Tom. Placing the coin back on the counter he picked up the drink and shuffled over to the bay window and sat down in his usual seat. The view from here was quite unique and looked out over the bluff and across to the Manacles.

A few days slipped by, and John finished reading the library books. Now armed with this knowledge, albeit only a glimpse of the past he was even more determined to find the underlying cause of the written records and the hearsay that in some cases conflicted. The discovery of the gold coin also led him to consider that a treasure may exist. Packing the books and coin into an oilskin bag to protect against the heavy rain that seemed to fall everlastingly in these parts he set off to the town.

Arriving early, he found refuge in the tearooms and ordered the celebrated crumbly scone with jam and a pot of tea. The wait was short but to John, it seemed frustratingly long. This time when the library opened, he would ensure his appearance was not dishevelled, hopefully saving his previous awkwardness. Moments later having entered the grand building, Miss Pascoe was keen to hear how successful John had been. He nodded enthusiastically. Miss Pascoe asked if any further books would be helpful. Knowing as much as he did, he was not sure whether further reading would advance his quest. He produced the coin and explained where it had been found. She was now intrigued and suggested that they meet after she finished work one day to go over his findings. John, thinking that all his birthdays had come at once, replied nervously

'Yes, yes that would nice'

Placing the books onto the trolley alongside the counter she told him that she finished at 4 p.m. most days and did not work Saturday or Sunday. Thanking her he began to turn and leave

'My name is Ruth'

This pleased him and he replied

'That's a lovely name, mine is John'

'I know, you told me when you joined the library'

They laughed together and he asked if she would like to come for Sunday lunch. Agreeing, she gave her usual little wave as he left, taking care not to trip this time. He thought his behaviour when in Ruth's company may have given her the impression, he was a bumbling fool, so now wanted to impress her with his professional approach to running the pub.

Back at the pub loud noises could be heard coming from the small inlet just along from the fishing harbour. Quickening his pace, he arrives to find the locals pushing out the long boat used for rescues when the lifeboat needed extra help when a catastrophe occurs. The sea was calm so there were no obvious reasons for the launch. The pub was due to open, so he continued home and thought no more of this event.

The evening started quietly, and many regulars were absent. Mrs. Emmin had mentioned something earlier when she had arrived, but it had not registered with John. Now though it was obvious something wasn't right as only two customers were supping ale, whereas normally by 7 o'clock over 20 would be queueing to be served.

'What do you think has happened' asked John

Mrs. Emmin replied hesitantly 'It might be old man Pascoe and his brother' and picking up the pot from the fire continued to suggest that he was known for going out with his younger sibling to dive over the wrecks.

Just then the pub doors opened, and several men staggered to the bar. 'Ale' they called in unison. Their voices brought John forward and he began pouring from the barrel as many tankards as he could before it ran dry. A wedge was knocked under the back of the barrel. The ale flowed again until all were served.

His questioning began and if anything was behind their late arrivals. In a subdued manner and voice Aaron the butcher edges forward. He is known for his strength but now his body was consumed with pain from an accident at sea some months earlier.

'I tried, I really tried but the sea would not give up its hold on them'

John interrupted and wanted more detail, but Tom had now arrived and spoke urgently.

'Never mind that now just pour the ale'

He continued and offered to explain all later.

John was not happy as he looked around the pub for comment. Nothing came so he tapped another barrel and set up replacement drinks.

Later when many had left, he sat with Tom and resumed his inquiries. Tom explained that a small craft had been seen to have difficulties about 100 yards from the rocky beach. Two people had waved and shouted at those collecting kelp on the shoreline. When they realised help was needed and were about to summon some assistance claimed the boat appeared to move violently from side to side as if someone or something was holding the stern. The two onboard fell into the calm waters. The boat lifted high and came down upon these poor souls who didn't surface. The long boat had launched to seek out the bodies, but no trace was found.

John was horrified to hear this and wondered why such an event could take place. Tom looked him in the eye and spoke

'I warned them not to listen to an old story of treasure beneath the waves, but did they heed the warning?' and continued

'No, they were intent on salvaging everything the sea may still have to offer'

John cleared the empty glasses and declared he was closing early. Tom was the last to leave and he made no effort to continue the conversation. John went to bed with many questions unanswered.

A week passed and another Sunday arrived. John stoked up the fire in the kitchen and heated up lots of water. When ready he poured it into the tin bath placed in the middle of the room. Stripping off his clothes gradually eased himself into the bath. With wet hair and soap in his eyes, he was unaware that Mrs. Emmin had arrived. She had brought up a large family so was not fussed by seeing a naked man in a tin bath. Asking whether he wanted his back washed he shrieked aloud

'Who's there?'

'Only me John' she said candidly, picking up the bar of soap John had dropped.

'But you shouldn't be here for another hour'

'Well, I thought you were entertaining your new lady friend today, so I'd planned to get as much done around the kitchen. Then, I can watch the bar when you sit for your lunch'

Thinking for a while John remembered his promise to invite Ruth for lunch. The offer of looking after the pub, while he relaxed, was too attractive to decline.

'Yes, that will be fine, thank you'

He put his embarrassment to one side and asked Mrs. Emmin to call on Ruth and ask if she could make it today.

Grateful for this, he thanked her again and when the door was closed made haste to wash all over and rinse before she returned.

Opening time soon arrived and as the doors were flung back a motley group pressed themselves into the bar. Each one expecting to be served first called to John who took no account of who shouted loudest. After the initial orders were completed, John looked intently along the path for Ruth. Tom arrived at the pub and John helped him straight to his usual seat. Even with so many customers Tom's seat was always left empty; a recognition by the locals that he was held in good regard.

'Something's different today' Tom commented

'Different?' said John, oblivious to Tom's sarcasm

'Yes, something's different about the place, and you, you look different'

Mrs. Emmin, having overheard Tom's remarks pulled at John's elbow

'You get his ale and let us not waste time on Tom's humour'

Still not grasping the point, John went off to get the drink. After presenting the jug to Tom he went into the kitchen to assist Mrs. Emmin. She could not help but chuckle to herself as John dried the pots in the sink.

'Will someone tell me what the joke is?' he demanded

Hesitating for a second or two she calmly replied

'So, the spotless bar area, the rug on the floor without caked-on mud, you with a close shave and wearing a clean shirt hasn't got anything to do with it then?'

Thinking for a minute, he looks at her and chuckled as well.

'Best you get back in there in case you miss her' she warmly said nodding towards the door.

By one o'clock Ruth still had not arrived. Tom noticed how often John checked the pathway outside.

'So, the mystery guest isn't coming then?' he quipped

John did not want to make an issue of Ruth's invitation so shrugged his shoulders and sat down with Tom. Mrs. Emmin came over and gave John a jug of ale.

'I've taken the meat out of the oven to rest, and the potatoes are ready now, do you want me to serve you?'

John had treated himself and on the expectation of Ruth coming to a beautiful piece of beef. Not the usual scrag end of mutton that he offered his patrons.

Feeling disappointed, he reluctantly said

'Yes, I suppose so'

Tom noted this and in a concerned way said

'It's not my business, but you've obviously been let down'

John admitted who was expected and upon hearing this Tom changed the subject to avoid any further upset and asked

'How is your research going?'

John relayed all that he had discovered and made emphasis on the books he had read.

'Books only tell the half of it!' retorted Tom and continued

'I was a witness back then'

John was about to ask why he had never mentioned this before. But then, as the door opened, the scent of fresh summer flowers preceded Ruth as she entered and made her apologies for being late. John stood up quickly and knocked over his chair; not the impression he was hoping to make. Wiping the spilled ale off the table with the cuff of his coat, Tom suggested she join him. Looking at John for approval she graciously accepted as he picked up the fallen chair, allowing her to sit down. Excusing himself John fled to the kitchen. Mrs. Emmin had already seen her arrive so ushered him back to look after his guest. The meal was immediately served with a fine wine. Tom retreated to the kitchen and secured the beef bone, chewing it clean. Mrs. Emmin persuaded him to linger for a while so the two seated in the bay window could engage in a little romancing. They enjoyed each other's company and cooed over their empty plates for ages. Was this love in the making?

A loud banging on the bar counter summoned John from his intense conversation with Ruth. He had neglected his post long enough and several thirsty customers wanted their jugs replenished. With only a few minutes to closing time everyone wanted serving, so Mrs. Emmin helped clear the jostling crowd. John was not bothered whether the time went past the last orders as his attention was diverted to other more important things.

Tom seeing how Ruth had been left on her own returned to the table and immediately she noticed John's quest to find answers about the pub's history. He was reticent about digging up the past and cautioned her against finding things that were best left alone. Ruth casually brushed off the warning and added that her knowledge was extensive on local history and had already offered to help John seek out the truth of the last century.

After the pub had emptied, Mrs. Emmin busied herself in the kitchen and John settled down with Ruth and Tom. Offering to leave them both alone Tom started to stand up but was instructed to remain by Ruth who felt he could help with the examination of the facts. With topped up drinks they spoke in turn of what they knew. John started by recalling what he had read in the library books and repeated some of the rumours he had heard from locals. Ruth was more overt and referred to most of the rumours as being ridiculous. However, she continued to explain that some of them did have facts to support them.

One such rumour that could be proven was the death of the local vicar. He was found guilty of taking advantage of the poor of the parish by offering a decent burial for their departed loved ones. Paid for by public generosity he failed to bury these people in the way he had promised. The families thought the bodies were ceremoniously laid in the church crypt but after a sham service, the bodies were thrown into the old well at the back of the church. The vicar, not declaring the crypt was full kept the pretence going for many years. The problem he had not accounted for and was to be his downfall, was the contamination of the underground water supply after the new well was found to be the source of a cholera outbreak. An assistant to the vicar realized what was happening and reported him. The vicar was stoned to death by the many deceived families at the entrance to the crypt when they could not find their loved one's place of rest.

Tom interrupted Ruth's recollections and abruptly said

'Hypocrites the lot of them!' and continued

'They were all the same back then, no one was without infamy'

John asked him to explain but he sat looking out of the window and was reluctant to say anymore. Ruth insisted he could not make a claim and not substantiate it, pressing him to continue. He eventually spoke and described how difficult life had been years ago.

During the winter of 1825, a major tunnel collapse in the tin mines left dozens of women without a father for their many children.

'Nobody would understand how those unfortunate folks survived, some might consider it gruesome what they did'

'What do you mean?' John asked

Ruth interrupts and agrees with Tom that a misfortune had occurred around that time, but she knew of no practices that could be described as gruesome. Tom reminded her of the wrecking of passing ships that took place during the last century and implied that not all were acts of bad seamanship.

'Well, yes, it's well recorded that ships were drawn to the rocks by a few bad people laying false lights along the coast, but the stealing of the wreck's cargo did not qualify as gruesome'

'As you appear to know so much of these events, what did your records say happened to the crew of these stricken ships?' he asked cynically

Thinking for a moment she told him that a few had died at the mercy of the waves but everyone else was saved and eventually returned to their home port.

John has been listening throughout and added that he had seen five graves in the churchyard of some unfortunate sailors.

'Yes, that's true but only from one ship' quipped Tom.

Ruth thought for a moment and suggested it did seem a low number considering that dozens of ships floundered on the rocks. Tom waving his empty jug at John said

'You ought to consider the records again; whether the statements taken at the time about the survivors returning whence they came was true'

Topping up the jugs with ale John took his time to think about what Tom was implying. Back at the table, Ruth had already started to try and unpick what she now considered to be a possibility and asked Tom.

'So, what you're saying is that the poor wretches that did make it back to the shore were killed'

'Where is your proof?' asked John mockingly, as he placed the ale on the table.

Again, Tom turned and looked out of the window

'What can you see from here?' he asked them

They both replied that a clear view of the bluff and the dark blue sea beyond was visible.

Turning back to face them he hesitantly told them that as a young man just 15 years of age he had been given a key role; to be a lookout for ships that were close to the Manacles. Alerting the landlord, who dispatched runners to bring together the locals to be at the ready.

'Ready for what?' John asked naively

Ruth knew straight away what Tom was saying and spoke

'So, you played a part in the mischief?'

John still had not got the message and kept listening with intent. Mrs. Emmin called from the kitchen

'I'll be off now, John'

Not realising she was still about he asked her to come into the bar.

'Do you remember much about the wrecking that went on along this coast?' asked Tom

'No, not the wrecking but I do remember my father was always bringing home lots of fine goods that he'd found on the beach after a storm'

'What sort of things?' asked Ruth

'Well, there were utensils for the kitchen, men's clothing, and timber for the fire'

'Anything else? asked Tom anxiously

Thinking for a moment she replied

'Ah yes, there was the meat, Mother would store it in the salt barrel, it was a welcome change to fish'

Tom stood up and made his apologies for boring everyone with his tales of yore and what did it matter anyhow.

After he had left with Mrs. Emmin, John and Ruth went through to the kitchen. With no clearing up to do they topped up the teapot from the kettle perched on the top of the fire and sat facing each other.

'What did you think of Tom, then?' asked John

'Well, he's certainly got away with him' as she poured the tea

'Almost believable, one might say'

'Yes, what if such things could actually be true' John said excited at the prospect.

They continued for some time debating the possibilities and whether Tom's account was plausible. He had shown reluctance throughout to discuss the past and when Mrs. Emmin mentioned the meat her mother salted, he abruptly left. There was something worth investigating and they both agreed to pursue the matter. Thanking him for the meal and the stimulating conversation she made her way to the front door. Giving him a kiss on the cheek, she suggested another meeting

'Maybe next Friday, it's a half day at the library'

'Yes, that sounds good to me' John stuttered, still reeling from the unexpected kiss.

She waved him farewell and was soon out of sight.

Part 3

Over the following weeks, Ruth spent a lot of time with John going over her findings. He didn't much care for the past now and used the time to impress her with the virtues of marriage and how he would like to settle down. Ruth had grown very fond of John, and she became very close, often staying overnight. Apart from the usual meetings at the library, they went on expeditions around the area.

On one occasion they managed to get cover for the library and the pub so were able to spend all day together on a boat trip. The mackerel they caught was the shiniest John had ever seen. Ruth had always liked the fish and looked forward to eating it later with John. On the journey back to the pub Ruth remembered something she'd read in her research and recollected that a small boat not unlike the one they had been out on, had frequented the coastline around the Manacles for many years. The sightings of a large, bearded man wearing a three-cornered hat had been heard calling out across the waves. The story went on to describe his apparent disappearance when anyone got close to him, the boat dissolving into thin air. Rumours followed the recorded sightings, and it was suggested that the strange apparition was a long-lost mariner searching for his ship.

Later, back at the pub, John was taking full advantage of having someone else run the pub and sat at ease with Ruth in the bay window. Tom arrived and congratulated them on the day's successful fishing. The mackerel was eaten without comment from Ruth, but it was Tom who asked for more. At the end of the meal, Ruth repeated what she had discovered in her research to Tom. At hearing this and holding his jug halfway up to his mouth, froze, neither drinking the ale nor putting the jug back on the table. John shook him on the shoulder, and he placed the jug down.

'Are you alright?' Ruth asked, now quite worried that she had upset him.

Tom hesitated for a moment and explained he had also seen the man in the boat.

'A ghost, it was a ghost for sure' he added in a state of apparent fear.

Unusually, Tom was now forthcoming with his memories and relayed a lot about those dark days. Wrecking was the only means of support for many families. The land was poor and only a few sheep could graze, that was if they didn't fall over the cliff edge or were stolen to feed hungry mouths from neighbouring villages. Jobs were almost non-existent; the local mine owner only wanted the fit young men to toil away underground. Fatal accidents in the mine were commonplace with many young women and their kin left to fend for themselves. Passing ships caught out by the intense winds and crashing upon the Manacles became the only opportunity to survive the harsh winters. The ships brought everything that the community needed; food was highly prized along with salvage that could be bartered.

Turning to Ruth he apologized for not saying anything before but as he was the last living witness to the crimes, he thought it was better not to worry her.

'So, the rumours are true, then?' John said in amazement

'Yes, they're all true' confirmed Tom.

'That doesn't account for your shock on hearing about the man in the boat; the ghost as you called him' she said provoking him to answer.

Tom went on to explain that it was a frequent practice to kill the survivors of the stricken ship so nobody could tell of the gruesome activities that followed the ship's demise. Still not convinced that he was being truthful they listened intently to Tom describe the women's role in the disposal of the sailors' bodies. They cut the flesh from the dead and preserved it in salt for use during the winter months. Both looked at each other and remembered what Mrs. Emmin had once recalled from her own childhood. Now thinking that this was all a tall story to bring in the tourists they continued to humour Tom.

'But what about the ghost?' she said scornfully.

'Yes, the ghost' Tom replied as he moved forward.

'You see the man in the boat is Captain Caleb Williams of The Peregrine'

John was looking confused and asked him to explain why he used the term -is- instead of -was- the captain.

Ruth had realized why already and said to them both

'Because he is not at peace yet'

Tom nodded and finished the last of his ale in one swig.

John announced he needed something stronger to drink as this was all too much to take in and went to the bar for a bottle of rum. Tom continued to recall to Ruth what he'd witnessed and explained the daytime wrecks were different. The crew from these ships were rescued and then taken to a haven and the cargo was left to wash away with the tide. This ensured that the night wrecking could continue without question as it was assumed by the townspeople that all shipwrecks were treated the same.

John returned and sat down again. Tom resumed his chronicle and told of the ghost that is often seen on the anniversary of the night The Peregrine went down. It is thought that the captain returns to look for his lost crew and his treasure. Interrupting, John asks him to tell them about the treasure.

'Was it gold?'

'Yes, it was gold, a chest full by all accounts'

Humouring Tom further John asked if any proof existed on the whereabouts of the golden treasure. Tom claimed he didn't know but added that a curse was on the treasure and anyone who sought it would meet with a premature death. Ruth remembered something else about the ghost in the boat. She told them that the same ghostly figure had been seen in the pub a few times and then suddenly stopped.

'Yes, that will be when they blocked up the cellar' said Tom and continued to explain that there were two cellars. John thought there was only the one at the rear where the beer was kept, but no, another did exist at the front.

'So how do you get into it, then?' John asked scathingly
'You're sitting on it' Tom said laughingly
'On what?' asked Ruth, now bemused as John
'There's a trapdoor under this table'

John stands up and seeing no evidence of the door beneath the table accuses Tom of winding them up. Ruth by this time had heard enough and declared she was leaving. Picking up her coat she asked them to forgive her, and she left.

John was disappointed at her leaving as abruptly as he'd hoped to spend the last hour or so privately in the back room after the pub closed. Tom, still smiling also left. John locked the front door to the pub and poured himself another Rum to carry up to bed with. He'd been taken in by Tom and kicked himself at the thought.

The next day John busied himself around the pub and soon after he opened for the lunchtime session another regular customer named Peter ordered his drink and mentioned how he'd overheard John and his company last night.

'Didn't mean to listen but hearing about the ghost did remind me of my father; he and a few others had to brick up the old cellar after it was claimed that it resided therein'

John couldn't believe his ears.

'So, there is another cellar?'
'Yes, it's under the bar'

After the pub closed John inspected the well-worn floor for access and found nothing except a square groove in the bay window. Fetching a lamp from the hook by the bar shone the light down as close as he could and scratching the dirt away exposed a rusty hinge. This was the trapdoor he'd dismissed so readily. With the blade of his trusty knife, he cleaned the groove around the edge of the door and revealed a small recess, obviously used as a means of lifting it up. All his efforts to gain access were denied as he pulled and strained himself. Deciding to wait until later he poured some oil over the hinges to soak in and hopefully release the trapdoor more easily.

The afternoon soon passed and having tried unsuccessfully once more, replaced the table, and opened for the evening trade. Neither Tom nor Peter came in that night, so John waited patiently for closing time. Clearing up the bar quickly, he attempted to gain access to the old cellar again. With a lever and using all the strength he could muster John managed to lift the trapdoor a little; then adjusting his position used both hands to grab the door pulling it fully open.

Wedging it with a chair, he climbed down the steps and with a lamp held high was overjoyed to see a vast room. Reaching the bottom, the feeling of excitement was dispelled by the cold and dampness that now chilled him. Turning the lamp up brighter, he surveyed the floor and then around the walls. Remarkably clear of rubbish it did have a thick layer of dust which stirred up as he walked across the room leaving a low cloud around his feet.

On the wall facing him was a large and heavy wooden rack supporting a few bottles. Picking one up and blowing its label clean began to read it; the dust annoyed his nostrils and he sneezed. The contents were described as Corbiere Rouge and holding it in front of the lamp could see it was a red wine. Replacing it on the rack, he walked further and discovered the wall that Peter told him was blocked up.

The stale air was now affecting him and not wanting to remain decided to return to the bar. Picking up the bottle again, began to climb the staircase. When halfway up, a creaking noise alerted him to the movement beneath his feet. Aware that the stairs were rickety he held tightly to the handrail. Unfortunately, this proved lacking, and John fell backward as the timber gave way. He landed on the floor below and was stunned as he banged his head. The staircase now descended on top of him, entrapping his legs.

As he regained consciousness the realisation that he couldn't move set in. The lamp had survived and still shone but now had a negligible effect as the dust cloud filled the room. Broken glass surrounded his bruised limbs, and an intense smell of vinegar burnt his already troubled nostrils. A sharp pain began to occur in his shoulder and upon feeling it with his free hand knew something was wrong. Blood was pouring from a wound; a shard of glass from the smashed bottle had pierced his skin. Time ebbed away and eventually the lamp expired leaving him in complete darkness as he slipped into a light sleep.

Later, he awoke to the sound of a scratching noise. Then, a tickling sensation irritated the back of his neck, and reaching over felt the warmth of a furry animal, a rat. It had been licking his open cut and savouring the blood that still seeped from his wound. Shouting, he brushed it away and now fully awake realized he was doomed. A saviour was needed but how would they know he was down here?

Contemplating his rescue, he looked up towards the trapdoor and to his dismay could see that it had fallen shut when the stairs gave way. This hopeless problem aroused many soul-searching thoughts as he lay helpless. His wasteful life flashed before him and he reflected on what things might have been like if his curiosity hadn't got the better of him. Weak from his injuries and loss of blood he soon passed out again and remained in this state for many hours.

The sound of banging woke him, and he could hear muffled voices demanding that he opened the door; it must be noon he thought. He called out but they didn't hear him. Eventually, the banging stopped, and he began to despair that this would be his tomb. Several times in the past he was unable to open on time and the locals went away, only returning for the next session. This meant they would not be back until six o'clock this evening. He felt he wouldn't last till then, so made his peace with his God and lay there waiting for death to take him.

In his weakened state he began to imagine Tom was calling to him, but it couldn't be so. The doors to the pub were impregnable and the rest of the building was built like a fortress, so they wouldn't get in to save him. Then, as all hope had gone, a digging sound followed by men talking emanated around the room. In the darkness, he was unable to locate its source but sensed his rescue might be imminent.

Eventually, a chink appeared in the brickwork and a shaft of light threw shadows across the room. They danced for ages and steadily disappeared as sunlight filled the cavity. A man he'd never met before climbed through and reassured him. Tom followed with several other men and John declared they were a welcome sight. They soon cleared away the timber and released his numb legs. Lifting him up they carried him through the hole in the wall and stumbling on the rubble from the dig managed to set him down on a blanket in the yard. Megan the local herbalist checked him over and confirmed he was not at death's door and would make a good recovery when his strength returned. To this end, she would fetch him something later.

Tom, unfazed by these events had already realized that getting into the pub was going to be a problem so gathered up an assortment of tools and a ladder to return to the cellar and attempt to climb back into the bar. Although crippled by arthritis, Tom was able to re-enter the pub and open its front doors. John staggered through them and into the back room, collapsing into his favourite armchair.

'Didn't think I'd see this again' he said thankfully

'Well, I'm not saying anything' said Tom scathingly

John knew why he was annoyed with him. The times Tom had warned him not to pursue the matter of the treasure were many so John changed the subject.

'Help yourselves to anything in the bar; the drinks are on the house'

Most of the men thanked him and left, only a few remained to take up the offer. Tom placed a kettle on the fire which still had some smouldering embers. Feeding it with another log he turned to John.

'You had a lucky escape young man'

John smiled at him and didn't reply.

'Yes, this time you did, but who knows next time'

John seeing the mood he was in and not wanting to offend his liberator agrees not to continue with the search.

'Be it on your head if you do'

They sat for a while talking until Megan returned and prepared a poultice for his bruise by warming it in some water from the kettle. A handful of leaves wrapped around the wound in his shoulder, held in place by a long ribbon gave almost immediate relief to his pain. With the water now boiling, a pot of tea was brewed and all three sat quietly enjoying a good outcome. Megan was the first to break the silence and asked Tom how his aching bones were after all the effort he'd put into the rescue. Not one to dwell on ill health matters told her he was fine. She went on to ask John why he was in the old cellar and how he knew it was there. Tom admitted it was his fault in telling him but added he had cautioned John not to act on the knowledge.

When the evening came Tom opened the bar and Megan went home. Many locals called bye throughout the evening, some for a drink and some just to ask after John. As the pub emptied early, the doors were closed but not locked as Megan was due back, having offered to return to clean up the bar. Sitting in the kitchen, huddled in front of the fire, Tom opened the conversation by accepting it was human nature to be curious about stories of lost treasure and told John

'You are no different to those who have gone before'

'What do you mean?'

'I told you that those who seek the treasure will meet an untimely death and you asked for proof'

'That's right but you gave no proof'

'Well, I didn't tell you everything, I was hoping my warnings would be enough for you to not pursue the matter'

'So, what haven't you told me?'

John was quite indignant now and Tom explained the proof did exist, but his father never spoke of its location. Hundreds of bodies must have disappeared over those troubled times but where they were remained a mystery. Some people thought they may be in the churchyard, as often could be heard crying between the gravestones. Others claimed it was just overactive imaginations and the wind playing tricks.

'What do you think happened to them?' asked John

'Well, if they were in the graveyard, I think there would be little room left for those who had passed in recent times'

'So, what you are saying is they must be somewhere else'

'That's a probability' said Tom shrugging his shoulders.

Megan arrived and started cleaning. Tom made another pot of tea and soon they were all sat talking. Megan hadn't been born when all these terrible things were supposed to have happened. Her opinion was asked, and she made no secret of the fact that local folklore had always frightened her. As a child she often called to play with the previous landlord's daughter called Teresa and between them had seen the ghost on several occasions: in the pub and on the cliff top. He tried to speak to them and waved his arms at them as they ran away.

'So, what did he want to say then?' asked John

'Didn't stay around to find out, but when we looked back, he was gone'

'Did anyone else see him?' asked Tom

'No, I don't think so'

As they sat contemplating what Megan had revealed they felt the room go cold and a previously locked window blew open. Jumping up, John stumbled across and closed the fastener. Megan put down her cup and glanced around the room; her relaxed mood was now overtaken by uncertainty. Putting her coat on quickly made for the door and in the blink of an eye she was gone.

'I'll call again if you want'

'If you are all right about it, I will make sure you are paid for your trouble'

'Yes, I'm all right about it but I don't want to hear any more of ghosts'
'Neither do I,' said Tom

John nodded in agreement, and they all went through to the bar. Waving them goodbye John locked the front door and went off to bed.

A week passes and John being a logical person and not bothered by the rumours decided that he would open the old cellar. It didn't take long, 4 days to the point of him cutting the final pieces of timber to complete the staircase. When clear of rubbish and swept out, the cellar was now ready for its first delivery. Bringing the wine cellar back into use would be a clever idea as the draymen who delivered his beer would be grateful not having to navigate through the bar and down into the other cellar. As for the Captain's curse, he considered the townsfolk to be stuck in the past and they needed to move into the modern world.

Sitting on the bottom step of the new staircase holding a jug of ale high in the air he congratulated himself on a job well done. His eyes looked around the space he'd created and thought the layout was exactly right. The new barrels could go over there he thought and the empties near the door to the yard. Then he noticed a patch of stonework that didn't match the rest. Standing up and moving forward he could see the outline of another bricked-up door. Could this be another part of the cellar, but why separate it from the remainder? He was still thinking about it when the locals hammered on the door; it was time to open.

Tom arrived soon after and John decided not to ask about the other bricked-up door. Having poured his ale and setting it down on the bar they spoke of how long the winter would last and whether John had seen Ruth lately. John had allowed all the recent events to cloud his thoughts and when the pub closed made haste into town to see her. After a prolonged apology for neglecting her, he asked her to call at the pub that same evening to spend some time with him. She had been aware of the accident and the discovery of the cellar so was keen to accept.

Later, they were both in the cellar and contemplating the advantage of having brought it back into use. Ruth also noticed the different brickwork that John had found earlier and asked him what he intended to do about it.

'Nothing' was his quick reply

She looked at him in disbelief and warned him not to do anything silly. Secretly he knew differently and felt compelled to explore this new temptation. After a long day at work, she was tired, so made her way back home soon after; not waiting for a meal. John was disappointed but realised he was expecting too much from her. The evening dragged until closing time and John was pleased when everyone had gone. He cleared up and went to bed. He'd already decided to wake early and investigate the bricked-up door so into sleep he went.

The bright early daylight crept through the bedroom and across his pillow. This woke him and soon he was dressed and downstairs. Putting on a kettle he ventured down into the cellar and with a small pick feverishly began to scrape away the loose mortar between the bricks. Eventually, several bricks were removed and the more he hacked at the wall the quicker the bricks fell away. Soon a large opening offered an invitation to enter the passage that was exposed.

With a lamp freshly filled with oil he stepped over the rubble and moved slowly into the void. The walls of the passage were solid rock and had obviously been hewn for a good reason. He could taste the damp and as he edged forward the ground began to shelve downwards; every few yards a shallow step took him deeper. The darkness was such that even the lamp struggled to shine a path ahead. Down and down John went until after a while he could hear the sea ahead. He knew what he'd found was a secret tunnel. Could this be one of the routes the locals managed to get up from the beach with their ill-gotten gains? The rumours were now becoming a reality and his thoughts turned to what else could be true. A moment later he saw a flickering light in the distance. It was quite a way off, so he hastened his pace and reached the end of the tunnel quickly. Huge rocks greeted him, and he climbed over them into the brightness. The shoreline was quite calm, but he could see the waves crashing over the Manacles only a short distance out to sea. How easy it would have been to plunder the ships that came upon the hidden reef below. It must be true he thought and sat down on a rock.

Time slipped by as he savoured what he'd found. He was the first person to discover this and revelled in it. Realising he'd been a long time down here started to make his way back. He knew Tom and Ruth would be amazed at this find and he couldn't wait to tell them. Taking his time returning to the pub he checked every nook and cranny as he went. About halfway along the passage, he came upon a fissure in the rock. It looked hand-hewn so leaning through the gap he held the lamp high. Its light was lost in the vast expanse it revealed so John turned it up to its fullest. What presented itself left him aghast and he dropped the lamp down into a crack in the rock. Cold gripped his body and in the darkness, he began to tremble. Running back to the safety of the pub seemed the obvious thing to do but what he thought he'd found urged him to stay.

Being a brave sort, he pushed his hand through and picked up the lamp, which still shone. Turning up his collar to shield some of the coldness he stepped through the gap. It took only moments for him to acquaint his eyes with the light and behold the walls were stacked with crates and barrels high above the water line. He laughed aloud and contemplated they contained riches beyond his dreams. He moved forward, stepping carefully to avoid the seawater that lingered at low tide beneath his feet.

After clambering up the rock face and with a little difficulty lifted the lid of a crate. The contents widened his smile and rummaging amongst the old clothes within pulled out a leather belt and a large cutlass.

'This will be a fine present for Tom' he said aloud

Still giddy from his find he descended and stepped onto a pile of what he thought was loose rocks. Looking down he saw they were bones, human bones. Mountains of them piled high. Hundreds of skeletons, some still clothed, some without a shred. How could he have been so stupid and naïve? This was the proof he wanted but now regretted wanting to find. He tried to walk over them, but his feet entangled themselves and he was brought down into the mire. He was now swimming in the remains of a dastardly deed. He struggled; using the cutlass to support himself crawled to the opening in the wall. As he found firm ground he looked back and realised many of the remains had missing parts, mostly legs, and arms. The stories of cannibalism were true.

Feeling sick he took one final look as the light in his lamp was failing. There in the shadows was a figure, a tall stout man dressed in sea fairing garb. As the figure moved forward John threw the cutlass and ran. Even without a light, he fumbled his way back; then slamming the trapdoor shut, pulled the table over it. Realizing the man hadn't followed finally retreated into the back room and collapsed into his favourite chair. But before he could evaluate his recent encounter with the ghost a noxious smell filled his nose and there on the fire was the kettle now devoid of water.

Feeling alone and still frightened ran outside. Looking down the path he saw a woman with her dog in the distance and waved to her, shouting. Either out of range or deaf, she did not reply. Her dog momentarily did turn and bark but then ran off further into town. Then, from out of nowhere came Tom. Never had a man been so welcome a sight as at that moment.

They returned to the pub and John poured a good measure of rum for them both. Tom had an inkling that something had happened and waited quietly for John to speak. John explained the events a few hours before. Now it was revealed, Tom had little sympathy. Leaning over the fire he picked up an ember from the grate and took several long sucks to bring life to his tobacco. Smoke surrounded him and then thoughtfully reminded John of the rumours about the captain and the curse. John shuddered at the thought of this and enquired whether just being in the tunnel and seeing the ghost was a threat?

'Not being a wrecker or in pursuit of the treasure should save you from a terrible end' Tom said as he sat down.

'Terrible end, what do you mean?

John now figured that the ghost may have thought he had been down there looking for the treasure.

'Well, it was suggested that those who sought the treasure met death after a while, some within hours, some within days, and a man who lived several years after claiming he'd seen the ghost lost his wife and child to a strange sickness, then he died in an accident which couldn't be accounted for'

Tom explained as he struggled to keep his pipe alight, taking further long drags on it. Continuing with his account Tom recalled the rumours one by one. The sightings stopped for a while after the wreaking finished at the end of the century. Only returning when the old tin mines were reworked near the pub. John had been listening all the time whilst he topped up the glasses with another drink.

'So, you think I'm safe then?' taking a large swig of rum.

Tom thought for a moment, then asked

'Do you still have that coin?'

'Yes, it's under the bar'

'Well, that's part of the treasure'

John stood up and collected the pouch and with the coin in his hand looked at it intently.

'So, all this time I had proof of the existence of the treasure'

Tom just smiled and spoke

'There my boy is proof that you didn't think that the existence of the captain's treasure was true'

John looked bemused

'Well, if you didn't associate the coin with the captain's treasure then you couldn't have sought it'

John sat down again and still looking at the coin asked how Tom knew this.

'Well as far as I am led to believe, that coin was found many years after the landlord died, many years ago. It had rolled under the bar when a casket the captain was clutching fell to the ground. It remained unnoticed and no one could account for it being there'

'But how do you know this?'

'My father was one of the people present when The Peregrine was plundered'

John was now quite incensed and asked why he'd not mentioned this all before. Tom explained that he'd taken the view that the fewer people poke into the past the better it was for everyone. But now with all this going on and the risk of the curse befalling John, it seemed the right thing to disclose.

Time moved on and the pub would soon open for business, so Tom thanked him for the rum and left. John followed him outside and as Tom disappeared along the path John could hear the wind picking up. Even from this distance away, he thought he could hear the voices of the dead calling him as the wind rushed between the gravestones. He turned and slammed the door behind him. Was this to be his torment, not knowing if the captain would come after him? Over the next few days John bricked up the tunnel and swore this would be the last time he would mention what he'd found and hoped this would bring an end to his fears, but would it?

Part 4

John had built up the pub's trade and carried out some improvements to the inside and the gardens. The bar area was brighter with cream paint on the walls and door frames; the doors were rubbed down and varnished. Outside in the old courtyard grass seed had been sown and created a place where families could bring their offspring. John had thought they could sit quietly on the stone wall consuming lemonade and an arrowroot biscuit. Unfortunately, the children did not see it that way and became a nuisance, accosting customers as they tried to enter the pub. Ruth understood their pranks and suggested to John that she would like a large family. He changed the subject and cleared the empty glasses.

Winter had settled over the land and seemed to last for ages. The usually cold and bitter winds swept through the area causing much damage. Wildlife suffered more than usual and birds that came to overwinter from distant places failed to appear. So, the coming of spring was a welcome change. Snuggled up in the kitchen one evening Ruth began prompting John to discuss names for children. John interrupted her and suggested they had plenty of time to think about that sort of thing. Ruth, however, had different ideas and told him to prepare the bedrooms for a new arrival. Looking at her sheepishly he asked what the hurry was.

'Well, I think you should know that I've missed for two months'

John being a bit slow in this regard just looked bemused.

Ruth smiled at him. Then the penny dropped.

'Oh, you mean ...'

Nudging his elbow, he almost fell off the seat and they began laughing until he kissed her on the lips and then thanked her.

'For what?' she asked

'For being here with me, for agreeing to marry me, and most of all for having my baby'

'Don't you mean our baby? she timidly whispered.

A tear appeared in the corner of his eye and upon seeing this she took the bottom of her of her apron to her own eyes as together they cried with happiness.

The next few days were spent organising a wedding and an announcement placed in the local paper. Ruth was to wear a simple outfit but an old lady that knew her from the library offered to make a dress befitting the occasion. It was delivered the day before the happy event but as this was several months since measurements were taken a last-minute adjustment was necessary due to the now-developing bump. Although having children out of wedlock was frowned upon this did not matter as they were the envy of all the singletons in the town.

This was a perfect match, and everyone turned out to see the happy couple make their way into the little church in the town. The ceremony went well and afterward their closest friends walked along the long and winding path back to the pub for a small and intimate reception. Unbeknown to them though, was a surprise from Tom. He and several of the regular drinkers at the pub had spent the last few hours decorating the outside and as the couple approached the sight was outstanding. Fresh white paint adorned the picket fencing, the path was covered in flower heads and the porch was draped in embroidered silk with the names of the newlyweds. It was surely a remarkable sight.

The celebrations went on for hours until around 9 o'clock Ruth went among some of them thanking everyone for the gifts and for attending. Then, giving a little wave to the rest pulled John's hand away from his drink and ushered him upstairs.

Tom stayed until late and then began collecting the jugs and wiping tables, thanking them one by one for coming. It was a subtle way of saying it was time to go home. Most got the message but a few well-oiled men at the bar asked for more ale, but the look Tom gave them as he placed a cloth over the barrel tap said enough. After the place was emptied, Tom tidied for a while, locked up, and left quietly by the back door. Looking back across the fields at the pub as he made his way home, he saw the dim light of the candle in the marital bedroom go out and so ended a perfect day.

The pub was closed for the remainder of the week allowing them some respite to settle into this new arrangement. Ruth had grand ideas and was soon outside preparing a patch of soil ready for planting. Doing it now was a clever idea as it would be difficult for her to bend in the months to come. John did offer to help but this was to be her little garden and he withdrew to the kitchen without argument.

As the months slipped by and she was unable to do much around the pub, John arranged for her to be taken down into the town by cart to see her friends at the library. Here, she continued researching the history of the town and the pub again. She found several references to cannibalism and when John heard of this, he tried to dissuade her from such a quest. He still had not told her of the tunnel or the sighting of the ghost. Just as well he thought as she would most certainly have wanted to see for herself.

Soon afterward a girl was born and with much discussion was named Mary after John's grandmother. She was a beautiful child with bright ginger hair and pale blue eyes. Things had not been good lately and money was tight as trade had dropped off, so they agreed not to have another child until things improved.

This was to be at least 5 years and Ruth duly became pregnant. After a difficult birth, a son arrived whom they named Michael. He was a small child and did not develop very well so the family was protective of him. Mary was given the role of minder when the pub was busy, and she took this very seriously. He was given the attic room to use as a playroom and spent much time with his sister playing there.

As time went by Mary became quiet and withdrawn. Ruth questioned her and discovered that she was having visions and could hear voices at night that upset her. Mary could not say what they were and refused to speak about them again. Ruth decided to brush the whole thing out of her mind and put it down to Mary hearing the stupid things that the drinkers in the pub used to say.

Now 6 years old, Michael started school in the town. Most days he was taken by Ruth and Mary but occasionally only with Mary. He was popular at school and soon allowed to have his little friends stay for the day at the pub. Mary did not always like this and was quite spiteful towards them. She had also started being in trouble at school and often hit other children in anger. She became an outcast and often refused to attend school. Spending many hours alone in the attic room.

It was during one such day when only Ruth was at the pub that Mary was heard having an argument with someone. Ruth rushed upstairs and as she approached the closed door; she overheard a man's voice. A deep gruff voice in a strange accent. Stopping and standing very still she listened for a moment before entering the room. The man was giving Mary instructions of some sort and she was pleading not to carry them out. At this, Ruth burst into the room and with raised arm was about to confront this stranger but only Mary was there. The man had disappeared into thin air. Denying that anyone had been there, Mary was told to stay out of the room in future.

Later, when told of this, John made little of it and suggested that matters should be monitored. Nothing happened in the next few weeks, so it was soon forgotten. Then, on a cold and stormy day, Ruth and John were summoned to the school during the afternoon. The teacher explained that Michael had been playing in the courtyard and produced a gold coin, telling everyone that a man had given it to him. Worried that it was stolen the school had decided to investigate. John explained that it was the coin he kept under the counter at the pub and would check when he returned home. In the meantime, the head teacher would keep the coin for safekeeping.

The next day John escorted the children to school and having wished them a good day of learning made for the head teacher's office. There he explained that the coin was not his as he had found his own still wrapped in its leather pouch at the pub. Leaving the school to figure out the origins of this mystery coin, he went home.

Later, when all were seated around the table Ruth asked Michael where he had found the coin, Mary prodded the little lad hard on the arm and he started to cry before he could answer. John stood up and shouted at Mary and sent her to her room.

'I'll deal with you later' he roared

Not arguing Mary left the room and closed the door behind her. Ruth comforted the lad and held him close to her breast. The question remained where he had found the coin.

John came close to them, placing his hand on Ruth's shoulder. In a quiet and measured voice, he asked the lad again. Pushing his mother away from him he stood up

'Well, I never stole it, if that's what you think' he announced defensively 'I only borrowed it'

Ruth looked at John. Then they both looked at Michael who had now sat down again and looked quite composed. Ruth was the first to ask the obvious

'You borrowed it, from whom?

Michael revealed that he had heard his sister talking to a man in the attic playroom. When he had asked his sister about this, she gave him the coin to look after, saying he could play with it but must not tell anyone about the man or the coin.

'I didn't mean to take it to school, but the other children didn't believe me when I told them I had some treasure'

Not wishing to call him a liar Ruth suggested he went to his room as well. Having heard this John did not want to pursue the matter and persuaded Ruth to put the whole thing behind them.

'Children, what imaginations they have' he said calmly, and he finished his jug of ale.

Not fully convinced Ruth wanted to talk further but John left the room in a rush.

The next day was Saturday, so they all went into town to have a treat at the teashop where John first set eyes on Ruth as she opened the library. Little did either of them realise then that it would lead to them getting married and having two lovely children. Cakes were eagerly consumed and washed down by several cups of tea: lemonade for the children. All their troubles disappeared from their thoughts and an enjoyable time was had by all.

After a short look around the town, they made their way back to the pub. As they approached something seemed not right and as they entered the pub by the back door it became apparent that someone had been in and made an awful mess throughout. Just then a noise came from the cellar and carefully John, now armed with a piece of stout wood taken from the grate descended into the darkness. Ruth scurried outside with the children for safety. Lighting a lamp John looked around and found nobody. The side door was open and there in the distance, he could make out the figures of two men running towards town.

After they had recovered from this fright John checked the whole pub but found nothing missing. Some rooms were in a mess, but others were untouched, so he concluded that they were interrupted in their crime.

'We must be more careful in future when we lock up'

said Ruth after she realised that the front door had not been bolted.

'It looks like we were lucky this time and yes, we must be more careful' John lamented.

When the pub closed that night, John sat alone in the kitchen; Ruth had retired earlier feeling unwell. Thinking about the gold coin given by Mary to her brother and the break-in at the pub, he was aware that something did not add up. Or did it? Knowing that a ghost did exist in the caves and the story of the massacre of the sailors was likely to be true then it was also possible that a treasure did exist.

Taking a lamp up into the attic room where this ghostly man appeared, he stood by the door and keenly looked at every element of the room. Nothing seemed obvious except the bed had been moved slightly. Placing the lamp on the floor he pulled the bed away from the wall. There he spied the loose panelling and with little effort slid his hand into the void beyond. Clutching the object within, pulled it out. To his surprise and delight found it was a small casket. Now sitting on the edge of the mattress he opened the casket to find bright yellow coins, lots of them, a king's ransom he thought.

Just then Mary came into the room and saw him rapidly closing the lid.

'You don't need to hide it from me' she said serenely

'I have always known it was there'

John still overcome from his find tells her to return to bed and they will talk tomorrow. This she did and he returned the casket back into the wall.

The next day the children went off to school as usual. Whilst at school Mary is playing with her brother when he asks her why his father was in the attic room last night. He had been woken by his sister leaving the room they shared.

'No reason' she said trying not to be bothered

'Was he after the treasure?'

She looked at him for a moment and asked herself how did he know about that?

'What treasure? she said trying to remain uninterested

He continued to describe everything that had transpired between the ghost and Mary. This concerned her and she needed to know if he had told anyone else.

'Seems like you know quite a lot' she said coyly

'Tell me, have you told anyone about my friend and his gold?'

Mary, thinking it was a well-kept secret now found that he had spoken to all his schoolmates and who initially thought it was just a tall story, were now convinced when he produced the coin at school. Now they all wanted to visit him at the pub so they could see the ghost.

Having learned that Michael had made it known about the treasure she considered how he should pay for his transgression. The next day after school, it was usual for her to escort him home safely on her own. On this occasion though, things would be different.

Later, Tom was to see the two children walking along the cliff path as he was out with his faithful companion Jed, a border collie with a pronounced limp, caused when caught in a wire snare intended for rabbits. Tom could also see a man dressed in thigh thigh-high boots and a three-cornered hat standing further along the path. At first, he thought nothing of it until the children stopped and began talking with him. Concerned for their safety he called to them, but he was too far away for them to hear. Tom made his way up the hill and eventually came across Mary walking towards the pub. She was alone. The man had gone and so had Michael.

'Where's the lad, Where's Michael?' he feverishly asked as he caught his breath.

'He's gone' she calmly said as she continued to walk on.

Tom staggered back along the path to the point where he had seen the man and Michael last. Looking in all directions he could not see either of them. It would be impossible not to see them as there was a clear view for some distance from this point. He knew something was not right and feared the worst. Tom hurried with great difficulty to the pub and raised the alarm.

John and Ruth ran back to the cliff. Calling out frantically they looked and with no reply leaned over the edge of the cliff. There below caught between two rocks was the crumpled body of the lad. Ruth was now hysterical and fell to her knees. Tom arrived after almost collapsing from all the exertion and tried to comfort her as John climbed down the precarious face of the cliff. Picking up the poor lad he made his way along the cobbled beach to the steps that led to the churchyard. John made the sombre journey carrying this sad wretch homeward. Placing the limp body on the kitchen table John took Tom outside. Ruth busied herself cleaning the dirt and seaweed off the only son she had.

'Tell me what went on up there? What wickedness has taken place?' pleaded John as he held Tom by the shoulders.

'It was the curse' he stuttered

Then continued to describe the man whom he knew as the ghost of Captain Caleb back to wreak revenge on any soul who interfered with his treasure. John realised he should have warned Ruth of any impending threat from this ancient mariner, being dead did not mean he was only a distant memory. He did exist and had beset this sanctuary called home.

Tom left to fetch the Doctor if only to make the lad's passing official. John returned to Ruth's side and gave comfort. Eventually, she cried herself into a half-sleep and he lifted her up off the floor and onto the couch, covering her with his coat. The pub closed for several days while funeral arrangements were made.

It was during this sad event when everyone was at the graveside that another break-in occurred back at the pub. They returned to find the back door hanging off its hinges. A search of the pub revealed all was as they left it; save the bed in the attic room had been moved. The treasure had gone. John had kept quiet about the captain, his treasure, and the curse upon it until now but needed to explain to Ruth how this awful situation had happened. He could not let this happen again if by accident anyone else fell into the clutches of Caleb. Ruth did not take the news very well and accused him of deceit and failure to protect the family. Her anger soon passed and knowing that the treasure had been taken wished the culprits would meet the same end as her poor boy.

In the weeks that followed Mary was not let out of their sight on the journey to and from school. The family's troubles did not stop though. The teachers reported that Mary was being bullied in the courtyard during playtime. They kept an eye on her but explained that she caused it by talking to herself all the time. The other children called her Mad Mary, and this created problems.

At home, Mary was no different and spent much time talking to herself or so it was assumed. The fact was she was talking with her friend the captain. Eventually, life returned to some normality. Ruth had spent a lot of time with Mary and now had a close relationship, sharing thoughts.

For one evening Mary sat cuddled up with Ruth in the kitchen. Ruth asked what she could remember the day Michael was found. Without hesitation, Mary admitted that her friend, Captain Caleb, told her to push him over the cliff edge for touching his treasure. Ruth was stunned into silence and said nothing. Later she told John of Mary's admission of guilt. He was unsure what to say and suggested they let the matter rest; they had lost one child and did not want to lose another.

On the following Friday John and Ruth stood outside the school gates waiting for Mary when a group of parents let off a huge cheer. Mrs. Tremaine the head teacher who was disliked by everyone was leaving after claiming she had been offered a new life up north. A large cart had been acquired to take their belongings with them.

As the teacher's husband loaded stuff onto the back of the cart the horse became unsettled by the crowd that now gathered to see them off. Seeing the horse was becoming more agitated he tried to pull at the reins to steady it. The horse had different ideas; it reared up and leaped forward. The cart lurched forward as well, letting the furniture on the back fall over the edge. The man hit out repeatedly at the horse with a strap and the horse in reply reared up again, but this time came crashing down on the man. As he lay there semi-conscious the horse moved forward and dragged the cart towards his body. The front wheel bounced over him and sent the cart upwards. The stuff that was placed beneath the foot rail now flew upwards and came down with a thud. A carefully wrapped object unravelled to expose a casket that fell at John's feet.

The teacher now distraught lay across her fallen husband announcing 'He's dead' my poor man's dead' and looking up at John she ranted on

'It's your fault, you and that box, take it, it's no use to me now'
Realising what the casket was, John picked it up and grasping Ruth's hand called to Mary to follow quickly.

On arrival at the pub, Mary went up to her room and Ruth pushed John into the kitchen

'Slow down, I can walk on my own' he said nervously

'I'll give you slow down; what do you think you're doing bringing that back here?' her tone was likened to a rabid dog who has just been kicked.

'I didn't think'

'You never do'

'Best I get rid then?' he asked, uncertain whether this would be enough to settle her mind.

'Do what you like but get it out of here'

Ruth pushed the kettle over the top of the fire as John made his move and slipped quietly out into the yard whereupon he met Tom dropping off some logs. Still uncertain what to do with the casket Tom suggested they bury it in Ruth's Garden. After collecting a shovel from the shed and with Tom's help, he managed to dig down at least 18 inches and placed the casket at the bottom. Pushing back the soil it was soon covered and out of sight. Tamping the ground with his boots he felt accomplished in this task. She would never dig that deep and never find it or so he hoped.

Bidding a farewell to Tom he gingerly returned to the kitchen and explained that the casket had been thrown over the cliff edge and would never bother them again. Ruth turned and having given him such a tough time earlier now reluctantly gave a sort of smile.

'Let that be an end to it then' she said bluntly.

John said nothing but gave her a kiss on her cheek by way of an apology. She elbowed him aside and placed two cups on the table.

'Suppose you want some tea then?' she was in no mood to be argued with, so John accepted and offered to pour.

'Do you want to bring more bad luck; I'll pour the tea'

she knew of many superstitions and considered this was one.

Part 5

The next three years passed quickly and with the dark days forgotten, life had moved on. Ruth and John had decided not to have any more children as the doctors warned against it following the difficult birth of Michael. Mary was never heard talking to her friend the captain again and normality seemed to exist. She attracted new friends at the school, mostly boys. They would loiter around outside the pub for hours in the hope of seeing Mary at the window. Sticking to her studies she remarked that there was plenty of time for boys later. This pleased Ruth who had feared that she would have problems with her behaviour as she became a teenager. But here was a near-model child, mostly pleasant, and a joy to be around. Nothing like old Mary who once was considered mad.

This idyllic life was soon to be shattered when it was announced on the radio that England wanted more volunteers to join up as the war with Germany was not going well. Although John was not expected to fight due to his eyesight failing, the other lads locally were finally called up to fight. Trade went down dramatically. Over the next 6 months, John began to reduce the opening times of the pub and did not open at all some lunchtimes.

As a family, they had to make ends meet, and growing their own vegetables became essential. Ruth would spend hours in the garden which now stretched to almost half an acre. Mary had avoided helping as she didn't want to get her hands dirty. After toiling for most of the day Ruth considered that Mary could help more in the garden. Calling John from his work in the shed she asked him to have a word with Mary and explain that she was a little selfish and needed to help. As usual, he did not make a decent job of this task and Mary did not come down from her room. Ruth was not happy but let the matter go.

Some days later the same thought about Mary not helping became an issue for Ruth. John was in town shopping for some meagre items that they could afford. Food was still plentiful but was very pricey. Ruth was not going to let the matter rest this time and burst into the kitchen, still in her muddy boots.

'Don't you think you should be out there in the garden helping to put food on the table?' she yelled at Mary.

Calmly, she replied

'I don't care if it upsets you, but I'm not cut out for that sort of thing'

Ruth threw down her gloves and slapped Mary across the face

'There, now look what you've made me do'

Ruth obviously regretted taking this action but before she could apologise, Mary ran up to her room. Ruth poured a large gin for herself and drank it down quickly.

Later, in the garden, Mary appeared and asked

'What time is daddy due back?'

Ruth was kneeling weeding with her back to her and only turned her head slightly to answer.

'Anytime now I hope, he's been gone ages, probably met up with his mates again'

Ruth resumed weeding and Mary stepped forward and picked up the shovel.

'Let me help'

Ruth upon hearing this was relieved that she had finally seen sense. Mary raised the shovel high above her and brought it down on her mother's head with such force that it split open, spilling her brains everywhere. Mary stood back and threw the shovel to the ground.

'That will teach her' she said, in a cold and unrepentant voice

'Yes, surely it will' came a man's voice from the doorway to the pub.

The stout figure of Captain Caleb was as bold as ever. Then without another word, he was gone. Some distance away Mary could see John stumbling along the path, laden with a large bag. He had obviously been drinking with his mates in town. Eventually after tripping several times, he came into the garden and on seeing Ruth's body splattered over the vegetables collapsed and fainted. Mary saw her opportunity and hurried into town to report that her father had returned from the pub in an awful rage and killed her mother.

The constabulary arrested John on Mary's evidence and even at the trial some months later he was unable to convince the jury of his innocence as his recollections were marred by the drunken state, he was found in. He was sentenced by the court to be hung by the neck the following week at the prison in Plymouth. Mary was sent to an orphanage and the pub was boarded up. Tom suspected foul play and decided to end this catalogue of death. He dug up the casket and at the next full moon took a small boat out to the edge of the Manacles.

'Take your treasure and torment this place no more' he shouted as he tossed the evil object into the swirling surf. Hastily he turned the boat about and made for the shore. When safely back on dry land Tom stood looking out whence, he had been and could hear laughter filling the night sky. Now shaking from his cold and wet body or with fear he returned home and locked the door. His midnight mission was complete and the evil that sought vengeance upon this place was now hopefully put to rest. Tom died several days later, not because of his actions with the casket but because old age finally got the better of him. The doctor who attended him as he lay gasping his last said at the time

'I'm surprised the old goat lasted this long maybe he'd a lot to do and needed the time to finish it'

He could not have been closer to the truth. Tom's final act was to be his finest and if the world knew of his bravery, they would owe him so much. But as it was the world never knew, just as well.

With the pub now boarded up the locals had no reason to go near the place except for the vandals that broke in and finished off the few remaining bottles of wine. The weather took its toll as well. Fierce winds lashed the coast and left a broken roof for seabirds to nest in, along with termites that ate merrily away at the timber floors without hindrance. After it was declared a derelict site, a local group took interest and gained official consent to renovate the pub; having been unable to find Mary, the only known heir to the property. Using volunteer labour, it was amazing how well it looked a month later. The group agreed that it should be marketed, and the proceeds used to benefit the poor locally. There were enough of those since many men had not returned from the war and those that did survive were either wounded or lost their minds so could not provide for their families. It was advertised and some people viewed it but an offer was never made so the pub was destined to be derelict once more.

The pub stood for several decades until another world war started, and it wasn't long before warships were frequenting the English Channel. Convoys set sail from all along the south coast. A few anchored just off the Manacles which was clearly marked on nautical maps now. Some perilously close leaving no passage between them and the shore. On a dark evening in late 1942 as the tide was high a sound of grinding could be heard followed by several loud ships' sirens and alarms. A vessel had found the rocks and its bow was now the only part showing out of the water.

As the tide turned and the sky brightened with the clouds breaking up to allow the moonlight through, a surprising sight came into view. A German U-boat had tried to creep up behind the assembled ships and failed to acknowledge the Manacles. The vessel was now surrounded by numerous small dinghies with armed personnel waiting for the U-boat crew to exit.

The hatch eventually opened and armed sub-mariners attempted to fight their way out but were soon defeated.

By now land based soldiers had lined the shore and prepared to take charge of these prisoners of war. Eventually, around 25 Officers and crew came on land. They were swiftly contained and were heard to shout in their mother tongue and broken English about the unexpected rocky outcrop that was their nemesis.

Months later, it was agreed the U-boat debris was unsalvageable as the surrounding rocks were too hazardous to attempt any recovery.

However, that wasn't the conclusion of the inhabitants of the local town. Meetings took place in quiet surroundings by the generation who remembered the old ways. There was no dispute; the wreck was to be investigated for anything that was of value. It had been speculated by many that U-boats were plundering ships they had disarmed before they sunk. The profits from this could be within easy reach. A small boat was dispatched with experienced divers to survey the wreck.

It was discovered that the sea had broken up the hull and was now spread over a vast area. Even close to the shore much was reported. So, the locals waited for a low tide and waded out with a small dinghy tethered to them. It wasn't long before smiles and hand-waiving indicated finds of worth to those patiently waiting on the shore. With a shared interest in anything found the men clustered around the goods and loaded them into the dinghies. They spent at least 5 hours until the tide turned and were waist-deep before their quest was halted. On land, the group was aided by more willing hands to move everything into the entrance to the caves. Without too much conversation they were back in the graveyard as was always the case back on the days when this night-time activity was a regular event.

Seasonal changes to the tides meant a limited opportunity would be available so for the next week or so the same operation took place. No sorting or sharing of the recovered goods was made until it was decided that enough had been recovered. It didn't mean the end of searching but any further explorations would have to wait until the weather improved.

A committee of elders was appointed to evaluate the findings and when completed would be shared according to need. Most locals were down on their luck, had no work, no prospects, and much poverty prevailed. When an assessment was concluded the highest-value items were agreed to be sold and the residue was shared among the poorest. Over the next few weeks, items were distributed and finally, the stuff to be sold was loaded up on two lorries and were to be driven miles away to Falmouth. Several reasons were considered for disposing away from the area. The best prices could be had and the risk of too many questions could be avoided.

The town of St. Keverne soon became a popular tourist centre. City dwellers looking for a weekend retreat brought many visitors in search of an idyllic spot in which to relax and enjoy the burgeoning sport of deep-sea diving. Attracted by the many wrecks that were scattered on the seabed. The rocky outcrop that made up the Manacles had become quite famous and was reputed to have untold amounts of artefacts buried beneath the waves.

It was for this reason that a young couple from London were house hunting and happened upon the old pub. Having fallen in love with the place investigated who owned the place. With the knowledge that the local parish council had compulsorily purchased it many years ago soon made an offer. While waiting for a response they stayed in the town and took in the local atmosphere. Few people could remember the old pub when it was open but did know that the landlord's wife was beaten to death and the husband hanged for the crime. As for the daughter she was never heard of again. This did not deter them from their desire to own the pub.

Eventually, the council agreed on the sale but stipulated it must be for residential use only and not used as a pub. Colin and Janis were ecstatic and over the following months spent a lot of time and money modernising the house. When at last they moved in they planned to go diving when the winter winds stirred up the seabed to reveal its secrets. As this was some time away, they busied themselves with local activities and made friends to socialize with. One such friend was the editor of the local newspaper and realising the history of the old pub told Peter about an article he had seen in the archives. He agreed to bring a copy the next time they met.

In the meantime, Colin walked down to the harbour jetty and took in the local gossip. It was a good place to meet the many-day fishermen that waited patiently with their boxes of smelly bait for the flotilla of small boats that worked the coastal waters. Most of the fishermen had started out early to partake in the fried breakfast at Mrs. Porter's Cafe. Greasy eggs, greasy bacon, and several other greasy delicacies on a cold plate left a congealed mess if not eaten quickly. All washed down with as much tea as could be drunk. After boarding they were usually hanging over the sides throwing up before they had left the safety of the harbour walls.

Later that day Colin met up with his friend the editor.

'I'm not sure I should show you this, you might get some fanciful ideas' as he hands him the newspaper cutting.

Colin reads it and begins smiling

'Wait until I show this to Janis' as he punched the air.

'I knew it, so don't blame me if any of it turns out to be true' came the stark warning.

They parted moments later, and Colin returned home. Janis was excited as predicted and asked Colin to make some arrangements to go treasure hunting.

The next day at the jetty he waited for the returning boats. The first to arrive had a successful trip and gave him some Pollock to take home for tea. Colin was not there for the fish but was pleased to receive them. Finally, he caught sight of the boat he wanted to see, The Starfish. A substantial size boat with all the modern radar and seabed searching equipment. Helping to haul the vessel up onto the pebbled beach he secured the rope on the instructions of the boatman. He thanked Colin and spoke

'You were born to it'

'Yes, I know a little of the ways of the sea' said Colin modestly and then asked if they could strike a deal.

With little hesitation, it was agreed.

Back home he opened the front door and announced his success to Janis who wrapped her arms around his neck and kissed him hard on the lips.

'Okay, we haven't found anything yet' he said

'Yes, I know but if we did, we could retire'

'Well, what that nurse said in that newspaper article didn't do her any good' Colin said scornfully

'Look, if she is right and the old man did tell her on his deathbed about a casket of gold, then I think we should at least try and find it'

'But what about the curse that goes with it?'

'Do you really believe that part of it?' and continued

'And don't think I'm going to eat that awful thing you've got in that bag, get rid of it and look in the oven'

As she went upstairs Colin opened the oven door and saw a half leg of lamb surrounded by nicely browning potatoes. Taking the fish outside and dumping it in the dustbin was not a problem as lamb always took first place on his list of favourite foods, although it did seem a waste.

A week later the weather was perfect at sea, so this was the ideal time for Colin and Janis. With all their equipment loaded into the boat they pushed off towards the Manacles. The boatman steered as close to the rocks and dropped anchor

'This should do you; there are plenty of wrecks showing on my equipment, so good luck'

The two prospectors smiled at each other and having tested their air supply slipped over the side into the murky water. They had not been down long when the weather started to deteriorate. The boatman fearing a storm was brewing tugged at the line to warn them below to return to the surface. From nowhere a small dingy appeared with a man at the oars and there in the distance, high on the bluff of the cliff stands a woman with a cloak pulled tight over her head and shoulders.

A dark ominous sky surrounds the vessel, and a vicious wind takes hold of the boat breaking the lifeline to the poor couple below, leaving them to the mercy of the deep. The cloaked figure folds back her hood to reveal the smiling face of Mary and the man in the dingy dissolved into the mist that now rolled in towards the shore.

Will this saga ever end?

Don't miss out!

Visit the website below and you can sign up to receive emails whenever H J BURGESS publishes a new book. There's no charge and no obligation.

https://books2read.com/r/B-A-AYLY-IEEJC

Connecting independent readers to independent writers.

Also by H J BURGESS

A Cornish Saga
Love and Belonging

Milton Keynes UK
Ingram Content Group UK Ltd.
UKHW041259011224
451929UK00004B/93